tiger tales
5 River Road, Suite 128, Wilton, CT 06897
Published in the United States 2020
Originally published in Great Britain 2020
by Little Tiger Press Ltd.
Text copyright © 2020 Ciara Gavin
Illustrations copyright © 2020 Tim Warnes
Visit Tim Warnes at www.timwarnes.com
ISBN-13: 978-1-68010-193-5
ISBN-10: 1-68010-193-5
Printed in China
LTP/1400/2938/1019

For more insight and activities, visit us at www.tigertalesbooks.com

For Caoilte and Aoibheanna
– C. G.

For Solar x
– T. W.

Weasel Is Worried

by Ciara Gavin

Illustrated by Tim Warnes

tiger tales

Weasel was minding his own business,
out collecting leaves,
when suddenly the weather changed.

He was **soaked** through
by a nasty rain.

Then a gust of wind
knocked him
FLAT on his bottom.

Weasel stood up and puffed out his chest.
"That's **ENOUGH** of that nonsense!"
he told the sky.

But just then the skies opened up,
and he was pelted by a mighty hail shower.

Weasel was starting to feel very small
and defenseless against this angry storm.

He built a wall to keep himself safe.
But the wind blew and whirled
around all night long.

So he built the **wall higher.**

But then the rain came back and wouldn't
take no for an answer.

So Weasel added a roof.
"Keep out!"
he said, satisfied.

Weasel settled down in his new safe place.
He thought of the storm raging outside,
and it made him shiver.

The days passed,
and Weasel got used
to being by himself.
But one day, he turned
around . . .

. . . and was alarmed to find Mole
sitting on his couch.

"What is this place?" asked Mole.

"It's a fort,"
said Weasel nervously.
"Oh, marvelous,"
nodded Mole.
"I love a good fort.
You guard this side, and
I'll guard that one."

"No!" said Weasel.

"It's not for playing in. It's a home."

"**Marvelous,**" yawned Mole, getting comfortable. "How about a snack?"

"**No!**" fretted Weasel.
"It's not a place for visitors!
It's a place to hide."

"**Marvelous,**"
said Mole.

"You count to
ten, and I'll hide.
No peeking!"

"No!" insisted Weasel.

"It's not for games!
It's for keeping me safe."

"Who's after you?" asked Mole. "Is it Fox? I'll help scare him away. Look at my **scary face.**"

"**No,**" groaned Weasel. "I'm hiding from the storm, and there isn't room for both of us."

"Well, where's the fun in that?" replied Mole.

"It's not meant to be fun!" cried Weasel. "**Just safe.**"

"Well, what's wrong with a good storm, anyway?" added Mole, placing a hand on Weasel's shoulder.

Weasel told Mole about the wind
and the rain, the damp and the chill,
the snow and the hail.
All the things that scared him the most.

"The storm is scary," sighed Weasel. "And much, much **bigger** than me."

"I see," said Mole gently.
"But storms can be a lot of fun, too!
Whenever it snows, I love to scoop it up
and make a snowman."

"And the **wind**," questioned Weasel, "that **knocks** you off your feet?"

"Oh, I love when that happens!" beamed Mole.

"The wind lifts my fur, and it feels all **ticklish**."

With a giggle, he **twirled** and fell over laughing.

"But the cold rain, Mole," continued Weasel.
"What do you do when you get caught in *that*?"

"Why, I splash around in the biggest puddles
I can find!" replied Mole.

"Then I sit in a chair by
the fire and dry off with a cup of hot soup.
Soup always tastes *extra* wonderful
when you've been out in the rain."

Mole had such a different
way of seeing things.

"But Mole," said Weasel,
"what do you do when you feel
afraid to face something?"

"I face it with a friend," smiled Mole.
And with that, he held out his hand.

Weasel took Mole's hand,
and together they walked out
into the warm, sunny day.